Grumpers' Farm

FARMYARD STORIES TO READ ALOUD

Other Collins Story Collections

THE SEA-BABY

and other Magical Stories to Read Aloud
ed. Susan Dickinson, illustrated by Peter Bailey

FOUR LITTLE SWANS AND A PRINCE

Ballet Stories to Read Aloud
Jean Richardson, illustrated by Amanda Harvey

Grumpers' Farm

FARMYARD STORIES TO READ ALOUD

Paul Heiney and Libby Purves
Illustrated by Penny Ives

Collins
An imprint of HarperCollins*Publishers*

First published in Great Britain by Collins in 1996
First published in paperback by Collins in 1997

Collins is an imprint of HarperCollins *Publishers* Ltd
77-85 Fulham Palace Road, Hammersmith, London, W6 8JB

1 3 5 7 9 8 6 4 2

Text copyright © Paul Heiney and Libby Purves 1996
Illustrations copyright © Penny Ives 1996

ISBN 0 00 675200 4

Printed and bound in Great Britain by Caledonian
International Book Manufacturing Ltd, Glasgow G64

Albert is a farmer who thinks that the old-fashioned ways are best. New-fangled ideas make him grumpy. Oliver, his son, is a farmer who thinks that modern ways are best. What makes *him* grumpy is the way his father likes to do things on the farm. But the animals at Grumpers' Farm aren't grumpy. They think it's funny having two farmers who argue all the time. It gives them plenty of stories to tell!

CONTENTS

THE NEW
RED
TRACTOR

THE NEW RED TRACTOR

Deep in a valley and way behind the times, there is a farm that everyone calls Grumpers' Farm. The father and son who work there are the grumpiest pair of farmers you could ever wish to meet. Ask anyone. They are not just a little bit tetchy, or even occasionally quite bad-tempered. They are, I am afraid, VERY GRUMPY ALL THE TIME.

Albert, who is seventy years old, thinks that the old-fashioned ways are best. He prefers the radio, which he calls the *wireless,* to the television. He doesn't believe in microwaves, and he thinks that a dirty old notebook is much more reliable than a computer any day. He also thinks that the old ways of farming are the best so he likes to use carthorses and not tractors. New-fangled ideas make *him* grumpy.

"I love my Suffolk Punches," he tells everyone who comes to the farm. "Big, strong horses they are. Lovely animals. There's no job on the farm they can't do."

"Except lay eggs," mutters his son Oliver, shuffling past with a bucket of swill for the pigs. Oliver has been to AGRICULTURAL COLLEGE, read all the latest magazines, and is about as up to date as any farmer could wish to be. What makes *him* grumpy is the way his father likes to do things on the farm. Mucky, old-fashioned ways! Oliver gets bad-tempered even thinking of them. When he gets angry his face turns as red as his hair. His glasses steam up and jiggle on his nose until he looks like a boiler about to explode.

Albert, on the other hand, screws up his face till he looks like a pig who has just bumped into a very heavy door. When they are both being grumpy at the same time, they do *not* make a pretty sight.

The animals at Grumpers' Farm are used to all this grumpiness – they think it's quite funny. Especially the day when Oliver wanted to spend nearly a thousand pounds on a machine to cut the long grass at the edge of the drive. The thought of spending *any* money at all made Albert very grumpy indeed. But the thought of spending nearly one thousand pounds made him fume. So he went out and borrowed a goat from a neighbour. He tethered it on a long piece of rope, and it tidied up the grass very nicely by eating it!

"Old-fashioned!" shouted Oliver in disgust. But Albert was very pleased with himself, and the goat was so happy that it broke its rope, just for fun, and charged at Oliver's bottom!

But, however old-fashioned Albert was, he did admit that when it came to getting jobs done, tractors *were* faster than horses, especially at ploughing. So he did let Oliver buy a tractor.

The day after the tractor arrived, Oliver was so happy that he was out ploughing at daybreak. "I won't be home for lunch," he shouted, climbing into the wonderful, clean, modern cab and fingering the controls lovingly.

Albert watched him go and

shouted, "Watch that old muddy bit of land when you're ploughing at the bottom of Six-acre Field. It's been raining. Even my horses find it difficult down there. You don't want to get stuck – it's very tricky down in that wet corner."

"Dad," said Oliver, with just a hint of grumpiness creeping into his voice, "this tractor has fifteen forward gears, differential lock, four-wheel-drive as well as a *seventy* horse-power engine. I don't think there's much chance of getting stuck anywhere, thank you very much."

So Oliver went ploughing and Albert settled in his chair by the fire. It was just starting to rain.

"A farmer ought to save his energy,

when it rains," Albert said to himself, and soon he was asleep.

The rain got heavier and heavier and still Albert slept. By the time he woke up, it was getting dark. There was no sign of Oliver or the shiny new tractor. Grumbling to himself, Albert thought he'd better go and look for him. He put on his very old overcoat and trudged through the farmyard and out into the fields. Every so often he shouted "Oliver!" but there was no reply.

Albert was getting wetter and... grumpier. He wished he was still asleep by the fireside. Then he heard a noise in the distance. He listened carefully. It sounded very like a shiny new tractor, with fifteen forward gears, differential lock, four-wheel-drive *and* seventy horse-power, revving its engine very hard but not getting any closer. Albert knew what had happened. The tractor was stuck in the mud at the bottom of Six-acre Field.

"I warned you," shouted Albert to Oliver when he got to the field. "There's more mud here than anywhere else on the farm. You are well and truly stuck and it serves you right."

"You never said it would be *this* bloomin' wet," grumped Oliver, whose face was covered in mud. It was a very sad sight. The brand–new, shiny red tractor was splattered with muck and had sunk so far into the wet soil that it was up to its axles in brown, gooey mud. And once a tractor is stuck, there is nothing it can do. Its wheels just spin on the spot and it sinks deeper into the mud.

"I don't know about mucky, old-fashioned ways!" said Albert unkindly. "You seem to have found a new-fangled way of getting even muckier!"

There was nothing they could do in the dark, so together they trudged home through the muddy fields. Albert was feeling grumpy at the thought of an extra job to do tomorrow, and Oliver was even grumpier because it looked as though his father had been right after all!

The next morning, Oliver was on the telephone as Albert came down for his breakfast.

"Who do you think you're telephoning, wasting money on phone calls?" said Albert, grumpily.

"I'm ringing a man with a large crane to lift the tractor out of the mud, and then another man with a crawler who can drag it off the field," replied Oliver.

"You're doing nothing of the sort!" said Albert. "We're wasting no more money on that tractor." He ripped the telephone plug out of the socket, put on his coat and marched to the stable where his three carthorses were standing. They were huge animals, with broad chests rippling with muscles, thick legs as stout as oak trees and coats that shone like golden conkers.

Albert took the harness and threw it around them. He was so quick they hardly knew what was happening.

"Come on Blossom, Captain and Titan! Let's get that tractor out of the mud, before that useless son of mine fixes the telephone and spends more of my money!"

He led the confused carthorses out across the fields. They were used to being at work, but not so early in the day. They'd never been over on this soggy side of the farm, especially when there had been so much rain.

Albert was muttering under his breath, "Tractors, bloomin' tractors." Then loudly, with determination in his voice, he shouted, "Come on Blossom, gee up old girl... Titan! Look lively."

When they arrived at the bogged-down tractor, Albert harnessed the horses three abreast and with a heavy chain coupled them to the front axle. He commanded them to stand still while he clambered up into the cab. He had never ridden on a tractor before and he certainly didn't know how to drive one!

"Somewhere this bloomin' thing will have a brake," he muttered. He pulled all the levers till he thought he had found the right one. It was cosy in the tractor cab, much warmer than in the cold, damp air outside. The seat was comfortable too. Far easier to sit on than the old machines Albert was used to. He leaned his head on the modern padded head-rest. "Just like a sofa!" he said. "Call this farming! Huh!" But he went on sitting there, and because he was an old man *and* he'd got up very early that morning, in two minutes Albert was asleep.

Outside the tractor cab, the horses stood obediently till one of them, Titan, suggested that something might be wrong.

"Well," said Blossom, the young mare, "he harnessed us on to this thing, so I suppose he wants it pulling. We might as well get on with it or we'll be late for our feed."

They all agreed. "All together now," said Titan and they leaned very slowly but strongly into their collars. The leather squeaked and groaned, the chains went tight, and as they inched forward the tractor came very, very slowly out of the mud.

"You know," said Titan, "we are far better at this sort of pulling than a tractor. Mud doesn't bother us. Our broad feet will always get a grip somehow."

"That's right," said Blossom, "and we can always lift our legs high out of the mud. Tractors can't do that."

They would have pulled the tractor all the way back to their stable if it hadn't been for a bump in the ground. Albert woke up with a start. He saw what the horses had done. He felt very pleased with them, and very pleased

with himself. "See!" he shouted to Oliver as they rolled up towards the farmyard. "Fully automatic, remote-controlled horses. Three horse-power and better than a tractor any day!"

Oliver's face went bright red, just like his hair. His glasses were steamed up and he was furious that his new tractor had been rescued by Albert's old horses.

"I think we'll sell this useless lump of tin," said Albert. "We might even buy another horse with the cash!" For the first time for as long as anyone could remember, his screwed-up old face broke into a smile.

Oliver's didn't.

Oliver *knew* the modern ways were the best and, under his breath,

he swore he would prove his father
wrong.

MANGO, THE GINGER PIG

Mango, the Ginger Pig

Mango, the ginger pig, was a favourite. Albert always said she would win prizes at a show, but he was too mean to spend money taking her to any. Mango lived apart from the other pigs, in a private sty.

Like all pigs, Mango could be lying in her sty looking as though she was fast asleep, but could hear every sound for miles around. She *always* heard the distant rattle of a feed bucket long before any other animal on the farm. If she listened *very* hard she could tell if the person who was carrying it was wearing rubber boots or ordinary shoes. If it was shoes it was bad news. It meant the bucket was not for her. *Nobody* with any sense would feed Mango the ginger pig unless they had stout rubber boots on. Her eating habits were not pretty!

Anyway, all day Mango would lie with her snout out of the sty, listening.

One day, she did not like what she heard. Oliver, the farmer's son, was talking about her.

"That bloomin' ginger pig is too fat. If she gets any fatter she'll be too lazy to feed her next lot of piglets. I'm going to do something about that greedy pig."

Mango lay perfectly still, as she always did when she is listening hard.

"She means no harm," said old Albert, "she just likes her feed."

"You're always going on about money," replied Oliver. "Well, I don't like wasting money on pig feed. I've found a way of making sure she gets her share, and no more."

Because it meant saving money, Albert agreed.

Up till now, Mango had shared a trough with the other pigs. It ran between her sty and theirs, but because she was bigger and wiser she always got twice her share of the food. Oliver had a plan to stop this.

The next morning, he arrived early with hammers, drills, wires and switches and set to work. By the time Mango realised what was happening, her sty had completely changed. Now, in order to get to her food, she had to walk through a metal cage, past a thing which looked like a camera, and then across a wobbly metal plate. She heard Oliver's voice, explaining to Albert how it worked.

"It's ever so simple, Dad. It's all connected to a computer. My friend at college rigged it up."

Mango did not like the sound of

this.

"When she walks through the gate, the camera lens will see something ginger and that will automatically start the computer. As she walks across the metal plate, the computer will measure how much she weighs and work out how much feed she should be given. The feed hopper door will open just long enough for the right amount of feed to flow out, then close. I've programmed it so that she can only have two feeds a day. It's dead simple! If she puts on weight, the computer gives her less to eat. That way we keep her just the right size."

Mango was suspicious, but it was breakfast-time. Nervously she moved forward till she was through the iron gate. There was a bleep as the camera recognised her ginger body and the computer switched on. She inched forward very carefully on to the metal plate. It sagged a little under her weight and went "ping" as it weighed her. Then there was a distant clunk and Mango heard the rattle of pig feed as it fell into the trough. She ambled over to take a look.

She couldn't believe it! Albert used to chuck in a whole bucketful; here there was hardly enough to fill a mug! How could she be expected to live on a ration like that? If it had just been a first course, with a main course and a jolly good pudding to follow, that would be reasonable. But this pathetic mugful was all she would get until evening! She put her snout in and sucked it up, then went back to her sty and thought. She remembered what young Oliver had said. If she put on weight, the computer would give her less feed. She thought for a little while. "If it gives me *less* when I'm fatter, then it will give me *more* if I get thinner." Mango had an idea.

Mango waited till tea-time when everyone was safely in the farmhouse before she called out to Mustard, the ginger cat.

"Psst, come here, cat."

Mustard did not like to argue with Mango. He could never forget that terrible night he had woken her while he was hunting mice in her sty. She said she would *sit* on him if he dared to disturb her again!

"I want you to do something for me," said Mango.

Mustard felt nervous.

"All I want you to do," said Mango, "is walk through that gate, past the camera, and over the metal plate. I just want to see what happens."

"Will it give me an electric shock?" said Mustard.

"It won't hurt you, I promise," said Mango. "If you do it, I'll let you catch mice in here whenever you want." Then she lowered her voice in a threatening way. "But if you *don't*, I'll sit on you!"

Mustard walked forward, slowly

and carefully.

The gate opened, and the lens recognised something ginger going through. It switched on the computer. Mustard stepped on to the iron plate, and there was a neat 'clunk' as it measured the cat's weight. It paused for while – as if in disbelief – then it checked the reading again. It wasn't at all heavy compared with the huge weight of Mango the pig. But the machine had been programmed to adjust the amount of feed to the weight of the animal going through. And so it did. When the feed hopper opened, out flowed enough feed for a dozen pigs!

Mango squealed and pranced around the sty gleefully. She had beaten Oliver and his machine. He would never be able to work out how she did it. She shot through the gate and started to gorge herself until she was almost bursting.

Mustard the ginger cat watched Mango, disgusted. Cats are very tidy eaters and know when they have had enough. They do *not* care for greedy animals, and they do *not* like to be bullied. Mustard decided to teach Mango a lesson.

While Mango was gorging herself at the trough, Mustard crept carefully back across the wobbly metal plate and inched forward very carefully till the camera could see him. Then he sprinted forward through the gate as

fast as he could. He heard a buzz and a clank. "Yes!" he cried as the iron gate started to shut. His plan had worked. The computer had detected something ginger, and thought that Mango the pig had eaten her feed and returned to her sty. So it automatically shut the gate and bolted it.

Mango, snout still in the trough, heard the lock turn and suddenly realised her plight. Now she couldn't get out. Until something ginger went past the lens of the camera and opened the gate again, she was a prisoner. Darkness fell, it was cold out in the open air and rain was starting to fall. Mango shivered, not only because she was cold; she was worried about what Oliver might do to her in the morning when he discovered she had outwitted his machine.

The next morning, Mustard came back. "Mango, if you say you are truly sorry and promise *never* to threaten to sit on me again, I will creep past the camera and let you out."

Mango did not like giving in. She just grunted.

"If you don't agree," said Mustard, "I shall leave you there till you become the hungriest, coldest pig in the world. Not only are you trapped, but you have had your ration of food and the computer will not give you another, ever. What's more, Oliver won't be very nice about it, either."

Mango thought this over. The cat was right. "All right," she grunted. "I shall be a better behaved pig from now on."

Mustard crept forward through the gate, heard the bolt clunk as the computer recognised a ginger creature passing the lens, and Mango leapt forward to freedom.

A week later, Mango the ginger pig was still behaving herself. She was not bullying Mustard. She was trotting past the lens. She was not eating more than her fair share and she was getting thinner all the time.

Oliver leant over the gate, looking at Mango. "You know," he said to old Albert, "that pig is getting thinner. What a clever machine I have invented. Science is a wonderful thing."

Mustard, the ginger cat, said nothing.

THE BIG
SPRING CLEAN

THE BIG SPRING CLEAN

Nobody on a farm likes flies. "Filthy things," said old Albert as he sat in the kitchen with a fly-swat. He was trying hard to keep them from devouring his slice of pork pie. He waited until one landed right on the top of the juiciest bit of crust and then he swiftly brought the swat down with enough force to swat a gorilla, let alone a fly.

But the flies were always faster than old Albert, and more often than not he hit a pickled onion by mistake. Sometimes one would go flying through the window like a tiddlywink and get as far as the pigsties. The pigs thought this was wonderful. They lined up with their mouths open, waiting for the flying pickled onions to drop from the sky.

Oliver didn't like flies either.

"I blame those mucky old pigs. That's where all the flies come from. The whole farm is far too mucky. It needs a good clean-out. I shall start on that tomorrow."

Albert was not really listening. He was watching a particularly huge fly. "I'll have you this time," he muttered as a fat buzzing bluebottle landed on his plate. He raised his swat high in the air and brought it down with a crash that could have been heard in the next village.

The pigs sprang to attention and opened their mouths wide. It was their lucky day. Albert hit the edge of a plate, and not only did the pickled onions go flying but so did two gherkins and a slice of bread. "Best hit yet," said the chief sow to her eldest piglet.

While Albert was trying to eat his lunch, Oliver decided he would draw up a plan to get the whole farm clean and tidy.

First he went to look at the pigs in their sties. "Filthy, stinking, muck!" he cried. "I'll dig all that old straw and muck out of those sheds tomorrow. Those pigs can sleep on a clean concrete floor."

Just as he was speaking, there was a clang on the tin roof. It was another pickled onion fresh from Albert's plate. The pigs stormed past, knocking him to the ground in their race for the onion. Oliver's mind was made up. He was going to fix those flies once and for all.

He stomped off to the stable and threw open the door waking the carthorses, Blossom, Captain and

Titan, from their midday snooze.

"Filthy! It's mucky in here too," he cried. "Look at the roof and the rafters. They're covered in mucky old cobwebs. Nothing but filth. I'm sweeping this place out tomorrow and we'll be rid of this filth forever."

Oliver turned and headed back to the house. A few seconds later a large lump of pickled cauliflower came whizzing through the air and landed exactly where he had been standing.

The carthorses stood for a moment, thinking about what Oliver had just said. It simply didn't make sense to them. They knew very well that the cobwebs were there to catch flies. That's why spiders spin webs in the first place – to catch flies. If Oliver swept away the cobwebs he would end up with more flies, not fewer. If there were *no* cobwebs in the stable, the flies would buzz straight from the pigsty, through the stable and into the farmhouse. Not only that, if there were no cobwebs to stop them, the flies would make life miserable for the horses. Horses hate flies. They make them itch and come out in sore lumps.

Blossom, Captain and Titan had to stop Oliver from sweeping away the cobwebs – but how were they going to do it?

That night, all the animals held a council of war. No one was happy about Oliver's plan. The pigs hated the idea of all their straw being taken away.

"Nice and cosy," they said. "All this mucky straw keeps us cool in the summer and warm in the winter. We certainly don't want to sleep on bare concrete. Anyway, it's not the straw that attracts the flies, it's the swill we eat."

"Well, can't you eat a bit more tidily?" suggested Titan the carthorse, "There wouldn't be any leftovers for the flies to feed on then, and they might go somewhere else, like the next farm down the lane."

The pigs just looked insulted at the very idea. "We're pigs!" they said. "We eat like pigs, OK?" And they refused to join in any further discussions.

"Then it's up to us," said Captain,

addressing the other two horses.

"If only we could get old Albert on our side, he'd understand," said Blossom.

Next morning, Oliver arrived in the stable with a broom, a hosepipe, a bottle of disinfectant, and a determined look on his face. Captain waited till Oliver had put down his cleaning tools and was about to turn on the hosepipe. Then, with one swift flick of his huge foot, he knocked over the broom.

"You are a great clumsy pest of a horse!" cried Oliver.

Pretending to be frightened by the tone of Oliver's voice, Captain started to jump around nervously, making as much noise with his huge feet as he possibly could.

Oliver went to pick up the broom and, as he did so, Blossom seized her chance. She took half a pace backwards and stood on the hosepipe. Oliver turned the water on at the tap but nothing came through. He held the hose up to his face, then stuck it in his ear to see if he could detect any gurgling sound. Just as he did, Blossom lifted her foot and the full force of the water sent Oliver reeling backwards until he tripped over a bale of hay and landed with his bottom in the bucket of strong disinfectant.

"Aggghh!"

The disinfectant was strong stuff, powerful enough to burn a hole in a

pair of trousers. And he was sitting in it. Luckily, when he staggered up, the hose twisted and sprayed a cooling stream on his backside.

Oliver was furious. His glasses steamed up with rage and his bright red hair was dripping wet. He looked like a fire someone had failed to put out. He shouted at the horses at the top of his voice. "You horrible, lousy, beastly, stinking, mucky, filthy…"

The stable door burst open. It was Albert, wanting to know what all the row was about.

"I'm trying to get this place cleaned up," screamed Oliver, scrambling to his feet. "I want to get rid of some of these filthy cobwebs and spruce the place up a bit."

"Get rid of cobwebs," spluttered Albert, "in a stable! You want to get rid of cobwebs! You young fool! Cobwebs are the horses' best friend. They'd be plagued with flies if there were no cobwebs in here. The poor animals would be stamping their feet all day, trying to frighten them off. Just think how many pairs of horseshoes they'd wear out doing that. Expensive horseshoes! Stupid idea! Didn't they teach you anything at college?"

Oliver picked up his broom and his bucket. He stomped off, muttering something about tractors not being bothered about flies. Old Albert pretended not to hear. He calmed the horses and reassured them that the cobwebs were here to stay, and they had nothing to fear. "All farms have flies. There's nothing anyone can do about it," he said.

It was lunchtime again. Albert went to the larder, got out a loaf, a huge sausage roll, and a big bottle of his favourite pickled onions and spread them out on his plate. The flies swooped. Swat! Whizz! went the first pickled onion, followed by a slice of tomato and a huge crust of bread.

The pigs woke up, stood in a line with their mouths open and waited for Albert's lunch to land. Captain, the carthorse, looked over the wall of the sty.

"You pigs owe us a favour," said

Captain, "and we shall not forget."

HORSES WITH HEADACHES

HORSES WITH HEADACHES

When Blossom the mare was no more than a filly, she used to get *terrible* headaches. And it was all because of the pigs!

Young Oliver got headaches too, but he *never* blamed this on the pigs.

He thought it was the carthorses' fault! He used to complain to his father, but old Albert had no sympathy for him.

"Too many newfangled thoughts. That's what's making your head ache. You can't catch a headache from a horse. Don't be daft."

So where did these headaches come from? Well, it was all to do with the summer.

The pigs at Grumpers' Farm didn't much like the long, hot days of summer, because they didn't like getting sunburnt. They longed for something to cool them down a bit, even when they were in the shade. The very best thing for them – as good as paddling in the sea might be to you or me – was to wallow in mud. Pigs love mud, and the hotter the weather, the more they love it. They roll in it till they have built a thick crust round their fat bodies, and then the sun can blaze down as much as it likes without bothering them.

So what has this got to do with headaches?

Well, to make mud the pigs first had to dig deep holes with their snouts. They did this partly to make lots of loose earth and partly because holes in the ground would stop the water trickling away when it was mixed with the loose earth to make mud.

The pigs at Grumpers' Farm used

to dig their holes near the water troughs. Then all they had to do was wait till no one was looking, get their snouts under the end of the trough, up-end it, then they had everything they needed to make lovely mud baths! Oliver and Albert had to keep refilling the troughs, which made them very grumpy. But that never bothered the pigs.

On very, very hot days – days so hot that even a thick coating of mud wasn't enough to shield them from the sun, the pigs made even bigger holes to wallow in. They started work in the early morning, just as the sun was up. By midday, when the sun was high in the sky, they had made a hole the size of a small lake and had filled it with water. Then they just wallowed in it. They rolled and rolled until they were covered, then rolled again. If they got hot, they rolled some more.

Pigs are heavy creatures, so their rolling in the mud packs the earth down, hard, in the hollows. When the summer is over, the pigs don't wallow any more and the holes dry up. Instead of being filled with lovely runny mud, they become hard, baked clay-encrusted pits in the field.

But what has all this to do with *headaches*?

Well, in the autumn, when the pigs moved back into their warm sties in the farmyard, the field had to be ploughed ready for a new crop. And every time the plough hit one of the hard patches, it was as if it had run into a block of concrete. And who pulled the plough – on old-fashioned, behind-the-times Grumpers' Farm? The horses did! And wouldn't you get a headache if you were bumping into lumps of concrete all day long?

Young Blossom *hated* ploughing fields where the pigs had been. Some parts of the field would be pleasant, soft land and the plough would glide through it as easily as a hot knife through butter. But when the plough came to one of those old pig wallows … Blossom shudders to think of it. She could feel the pain even years later. First of all there was a twang as the plough chains went tight. Then there was a creak as the full weight came on her collar. Then a terrible pain as she leant forward to pull the heavier load. It didn't take many of those before she had a splitting headache.

Oliver *hated* ploughing with horses so he never paid much attention to the horse or the land he was ploughing. He had his mind on other things – usually tractors – and got in a terrible temper if anything went wrong. But Blossom couldn't help getting her feet in the wrong place, or stepping out of line, when the plough hit one of these concrete-like wallows. No wonder she slowed up a bit. Oliver shouted at her, told her not to be so lazy and gradually got himself into such a temper that before long his hair went an even brighter red, his glasses steamed, and *his* head started to ache.

And that's how pigs give horses and people headaches.

It was easy for Oliver. He could take a headache pill. But poor old Blossom had no way of telling Oliver or old Albert that her head ached at the end of those terrible days ploughing the pig fields. She longed for a pill, but there was no chance of *her* getting one.

Captain and Titan, the other carthorses, started to worry about Blossom. She was getting more and more miserable at the thought of all the ploughing that still had to be done, and how much her head was going to ache. She got sadder and sadder, casting a heavy gloom around the stable.

Captain, the senior horse, decided it was time for action. "I want a word with you pigs," he snorted over the farmyard wall while the pigs were at their trough. The pigs didn't even look up, they just kept on eating, ignoring him.

Captain hatched a plot. Between the stables and the pigsty was a brick wall. As dusk fell and the pigs started to drop off to sleep, the horses took it in turns to lift one of their massive feet and give the wall a good, hefty kick. Just one kick. Then they let it go quiet again. They waited till the pigs had just drifted off to sleep again and SMASH! they struck the wall again. Then it went quiet. They did this all night for three nights. The horses were pretty tired by then, but not as tired as the pigs. Pigs need their sleep.

"Oink... Captain... grunt... What's all this noise in the night? We can't get any sleep... oink... We've all got terrible headaches," moaned Mango the ginger pig.

"Now you know what it's like to have a headache, you might have some sympathy for us," said Captain. "If you go out to those fields late one night and truffle through all those hard spots, soften them up a bit for us, we'll let you have your rest. Is it a deal?"

Pigs' noses are well designed for digging. They look soft and rubbery but they have great power in them. When a pig says it is going to get its nose stuck into something, it really means it. Mango once dug up half the concrete in her sty, just because she was bored.

The pigs finally agreed and the next night, when Oliver and Albert were fast asleep, Captain got out of his stable. With one kick he broke the catch of the pigsty door. "If anyone notices," he said to himself, "they'll think a feed lorry reversed into it."

The pigs crept out to the field under cover of darkness and truffled till their noses were nearly worn out. Then they went back to their sty and slept. During the day, they pretended the door was locked. It took them nearly a week to clear every field of hardened wallows, but they did it. All the hard, lumpy soil in the fields was broken up, the plough went through it easily and Blossom never got another headache.

Blossom started to enjoy her work again. She walked fast and in a perfect straight line and Oliver no longer needed to shout at her. His headaches went too, but he didn't know why.

Every autumn, the horses and the pigs do the same thing, and neither Oliver nor Albert has ever noticed. But Oliver did wonder where the headaches had gone. The other thing he couldn't understand was why the pigs seemed to need so much sleep during the day!

How Mangels made them Merry

HOW MANGELS
MADE THEM
MERRY

All the animals at Grumpers' Farm loved mangelwurzels. They were their very favourite thing.

Mangels look a bit like bright red rugby balls. They grow in the fields and have broad green leaves when they first sprout, but after a time a big, swollen root develops that gets bigger and bigger until it looks fit to burst. That's when Albert and Oliver harvest them and it's usually before the frost comes. Mangels don't like frost. They freeze and then turn mushy when they thaw – like cucumbers that have been in the fridge too long.

Mangels are very, very juicy and this is what the animals at Grumpers' Farm love best. But because mangels have so much juice in them, they're very easy to damage once lifted from the fields. If they get scratched or pierced, they weep and all the juiciness drains away.

Oliver hated harvesting mangels. He preferred things that you could handle quickly, and roughly. "If we grew some modern kind of fodder for the winter, we could get a machine to come and lift them, and save us doing it by hand," was his usual grumble.

"If we had modern fodder and one of those speedy machines," old Albert replied, "what would the horses do in November if there were no mangels to lift?"

Lifting the mangels took ages. Every one had to be pulled from the ground by hand and put into the cart, and when it was full the horses would haul it to the growing mangel mountain in a corner of the farmyard. When the mangels had all been lifted, Albert covered the mountain with straw to keep out the winter frosts.

Then came the worst bit – the waiting. If you were to taste a mangelwurzel in November, it would be very dull compared with the way it tastes by January. A great change takes place inside mangels during the winter. As the weeks go by, they get sweeter and sweeter and sweeter. By the time Christmas is over, eating a mangel is like chewing on a lump of sugar.

Mangels were usually a treat for the animals in winter, but one year, they weren't all that interested in them. The autumn had been mild and showery and they were quite happy to keep eating the grass on the meadow that had stayed as lush as if it had been spring. The mangels didn't seem so important and were left under the straw, almost forgotten.

Winter eventually arrived two months late. Cold winds blew, and the grass stopped growing. The animals got tired of chewing at dry straw. Mango, the ginger pig, was desperate for something juicy and so were the carthorses.

Mustard the cat, however, had a secret. He had been quietly sneaking under the straw covering the mangel-heap and having a good lick when no one was looking. He had decided not to tell the others what he had discovered.

"Brrrr, it's a chilly old day," Albert grumbled one day, winding his scarf round and round his neck until all you could see was a purple nose sticking out of a tangle of red wool. "I think getting the straw off that mangel heap is a job for a young 'un, Oliver!"

Oliver trudged off to the farmyard with his fork. He had only been out of the house five minutes and already his hands were frozen. When he got to the mangel heap, he noticed that, strangely, there was no frost on it. There was thick ice in the water troughs, frozen puddles in the yard and the cattle's steamy breath filled the air. But there was no frost on the mangel heap.

"I don't care," he muttered, "I want to get back indoors. I hate mangels."

He scraped away the thick layer of straw, and as he did so, a strong sweet smell swept over. He staggered back and fell on his bottom in the frozen mud.

He coughed, "Wow!"

Getting up, Oliver carefully went closer to have another sniff. The smell reminded him of something, but he could not remember quite what.

By now, the smell had spread across the farmyard. It was so good that the sheep started to bleat, the horses whinnied and the cows mooed.

Oliver stabbed his fork into the heap, filled a large barrow and then went on his rounds, giving mangels to all the animals. Their chewing was so loud, no other sound could be heard anywhere on the farm. And on the animals' faces were smiles of utter bliss. It was like a party, or the moment when the Christmas pudding is brought to the table smelling of fruit and brandy. Oliver went back to the house, glad to be out of the cold wind.

Later that evening, just as it was getting dark, he thought he ought to check everything was safely shut up for the night. First of all he went into the stable where the horses were standing. Everything looked fine, except for Blossom, who seemed to be swaying from side to side.

"Daft old horse, stand STILL," shouted Oliver. Blossom did her best to obey. In the darkness, Oliver thought he heard her hiccup.

Oliver went out of the stable into the yard and thought he heard an even odder sound coming from the sheep. It sounded like a chorus of belches and hiccups, with a strange baa-ing giggle that ended suddenly, as if the giggler had fallen over. Then there was another. Oliver looked round to see that his father had not followed him. Then it happened again.

Hiccup! BAA! Heeeheeehee! It *was* the sheep. Shocked, Oliver looked across to the other side of the yard and saw the cows. They had lined them selves up alongside each other, and were swaying gently. One of them started to moo and the others joined in. They were singing! They really were trying to sing and sway along with the rhythm. Oliver ran back to the house.

"Dad, get the vet. The whole farm

has got some terrible disease. All the animals have gone crazy. The sheep have got hiccups, the horses are swaying from side to side and the cows are singing in harmony!"

Albert put his coat on, wrapped his scarf round and round his neck and trudged across to the yard. He looked carefully at all the animals, peered into their eyes and smelt their breath.

"It is very serious," said Albert in a grave voice. Oliver looked very worried, fearing his father was about to break some bad news to him. Then Albert's face cracked and a huge smile came to his lips. "The animals are not ill, they're DRUNK!"

"It's not possible," said Oliver. "All they've had to drink is water!"

"And mangels," added Albert. "Pass one over here."

Albert split the mangel in half and sniffed long and hard. Then he ran his tongue over it. Another huge smile nearly cracked his face in half.

"Fermented. These mangels have fermented. They've been in that heap so long, all the sugar has started turning into alcohol. It's called fermentation. It's how they make wine, my boy. These animals have been drinking mangel wine!" he chortled.

"We must do something, urgently!" said Oliver.

"We shall," said Albert. "I shall take a couple straight into the house and sit by the fire sucking one. That will keep the cold out."

"And what about the animals?" said Oliver.

"They'll be fine," replied Albert, "but do be quiet when you feed them in the morning. They'll have terrible hangovers."

Witches at Grumpers' Farm

WITCHES AT GRUMPERS' FARM

No one would have believed it possible. The cows asked the pigs, "Do you think Farmer Albert really means what he just said?"

The pigs thought for a minute, just to make sure that their ears had not deceived them. "Yes," said Mango, the ginger pig, "I couldn't believe it either, but I am sure he said it."

Word spread round the farm like wildfire. The hens were cackling about it, the sheep bleated the news to each other over the soggy hedges. There was little else to talk about. It was the greatest news to hit the farm for years.

The only animals at Grumpers' Farm who could not bring themselves to discuss it were the carthorses, Blossom, Titan and Captain. They simply stood in their stalls, frozen in terror, unable to utter a word.

It was Blossom who finally broke the silence.

"Captain," she said under her breath, "do you think he means it?"

Captain thought for a moment and said, "I suppose he does."

Blossom started to tremble.

"Cheer up, old girl," said Titan. "It may not be as bad as we think." He said it as convincingly as he could manage, but all the same a great gloom fell over the stable.

What had happened was this. As usual at Grumpers' Farm, it all started with an argument between old Albert and young Oliver. Oliver had been shouting that the farm was old-fashioned, behind the times, and needed new machines and not slow old carthorses. "We're a joke!" he shouted. "Everyone laughs at us! We need to modernise!" There was nothing new about that; the animals had heard Oliver and Albert arguing like this for years on the subject.

But this time, to the surprise of everyone on the farm, old Albert's reply was different. Instead of fiercely arguing that horses were best, he gave in. Just like that. His very words were, "Oliver, my boy, I think you are RIGHT. The carthorses have had their day. It is time they went. We could use the stable as a shed for tractors."

Oliver reeled back, shocked. He felt as if he had been pushing on a locked door, and suddenly it had given way. He couldn't believe it.

"Of course," said Albert, "some people used to say that getting rid of horses brought bad luck on a farm – because witches protect the horses

from anyone trying to do them harm."
He chuckled. "But that's just a load of
old country nonsense. Don't you fret
about witches, boy."

"I certainly shall not," said Oliver
haughtily. "Witches do not feature in
modern farming methods. They didn't
teach us about witches at college.
Witches are none of my concern."

"That's quite right," said old
Albert. "It's just a load of old
nonsense. I wouldn't worry about it."

Oliver was already running back to
the house, to order the brand new
tractors he had longed for. He didn't
see the hint of a smile spreading across
old Albert's face.

That night, over supper, Albert started

talking about the witches again.

"I can tell you another thing about witches," he said, but Oliver didn't take much notice. His head was buried in a glossy catalogue of the very latest farming equipment.

Albert persisted. "They used to believe, in the old days…"

Oliver had heard those words so many times before that his ears were now closed to everything his father said.

"…that witches came in the night and rode the horses. That was the reason why you sometimes found a horse with a sweat on in the morning. That's true, that is!" said Albert.

Oliver nodded, but he had not been listening properly.

"The only way to keep the witches away from the horses was to hang a hag-stone in the stable. A hag-stone is a flint with a hole in it, like a mint. You find them in the fields if you keep your eyes open. There's one in the stable now."

"Dad," said Oliver, annoyed because he could not concentrate on his glossy catalogue. "You're talking a load of rubbish. There are no such things as witches, and hag-stones do not have special magic powers. Understand?"

"Oh, I'm sure you're right," said old Albert. "The hag-stone that hangs just above Blossom's manger, well, I'd throw that away if I were you." He paused. "Unless, of course, you do believe in witches."

"You're a mad old man," said Oliver unkindly, and went upstairs, clutching his catalogue.

But Oliver slept badly, dreaming of witches.

The next morning, to prove he did not believe in any of this old mumbo-jumbo, Oliver went to the stable, took the hag-stone off the hook, and flung it into the muck-heap. The carthorses watched him do it. Now they were really very worried. It looked as though their days were numbered.

That afternoon when Oliver had gone into town, Albert marched out to the farmyard. He took a bale of straw, stood on it, and like a major-general addressing his troops, made the following announcement.

"My dear friends at Grumpers' Farm. My dear animals. My beloved carthorses." His voice was breaking slightly with the emotion of the moment and tears welled in his eyes. "I know you think I have let you all down by giving in to young Oliver and his modern ways. But the truth is I'm fed up with this being the grumpiest farm that ever was. The only way to stop these arguments is for one of us to give in."

Pigs, sheep, hens, cattle and carthorses were stiff with attention.

"But things are not quite what they seem," Albert went on. "I have a plan, and if you will help me with it then we might put an end to all this talk of modern farming methods once and for all. Are you all with me?"

The animals looked at him and bleated, grunted, mooed, clucked and neighed their approval.

Later that night, Albert was sitting in front of the log fire listening to Oliver's new plans for the farm. He was also listening to small noises from the farmyard, and chuckling to himself.

In the stable, Blossom the carthorse wandered over to the water trough, and dipped her head deep into it. She flicked the water sharply backwards so that the spray covered her whole body. It looked just as if she were sweating all over. Then she started to stamp her feet, to make a sound as if she were galloping. This was all part of the plan.

Albert rose from his arm-chair and said to Oliver, "Terrible noise in the stable. Best see what's going on."

"I'll go Dad. Don't disturb yourself," said Oliver who was now feeling kindly towards his old dad.

Oliver went across to the stable and opened the door. The first thing he saw was Blossom in a sweat. Albert watched from the window and just as Oliver went inside the stable, he pulled the electric fuse out and plunged the entire farmyard into darkness.

Then it was the pig's turn. Mango, the ginger pig, had been instructed that as soon as the lights went out she was to make the most fearful noise she could imagine. Knowing that the entire future of the farm was at stake, she heroically ordered one of the other pigs to bite and twist her tail. Mango was not popular with the other pigs, so the pig took this opportunity to bite Mango's tail very hard indeed! Mango squealed in pain – a great, gasping, ghostly shriek fit to curdle anyone's blood. It cut through the pitch black night. Oliver leapt out of his skin, and spun round towards the glimmering light of the stable window.

To his horror, a ghostly white face appeared there, with horns like a devil. Mango gave another ghostly squeal. Oliver shrieked, almost as loud. Then

at exactly the same moment, the owl hooted from the rafters and the white bull ambled across from the window and rubbed his head against the door so that it rattled like thunder. Blossom pranced on the spot to add to the commotion.

By the time Oliver had found the door, and stumbled across the yard back to the house, he was trembling and was as white as a sheet.

"Dad, Dad!" he gasped. "Something's happening out there."

Albert did not stir, much.

"Not witches riding the horses, is it?" he said. "Don't suppose that hag-stone you threw away would make any difference." And he laughed. Oliver by now was in bed, his head buried deep under the duvet.

Next morning, when Oliver had finally stopped trembling, he went to the muck-heap with a big fork and dug deep till he found the hag-stone. Then he carefully hung it above Blossom and, without saying a word, began to groom the big horse.

"Best send for the lorry and get rid of these old horses," said Albert. Oliver quietly went on brushing Blossom. "Unless you're worried about the witches coming to haunt us?"

"Not at all," said Oliver. "But I think it can wait till next week."

But it never happened at all. Oliver

never argued with his father again. He took up computer programming and designed Efficiency Programmes for other farms, big farms. He became well-known as an expert on modern farming methods and he never let anyone find out that he lived on a farm where horses still worked the land.

Albert and Oliver never became rich, but they were both perfectly happy. So happy, in fact, that there was never any more grumpiness at Grumpers' Farm.